5937208871840 1   FTBC

WITHDRAWN
WORN, SOILED, OBSOLETE

D0516426

BY **JENNIFER HAMBURG**

ILLUSTRATED BY **EDWIN FOTHERINGHAM**

MONKEY AND DUCK QUACK UP!

SCHOLASTIC PRESS | NEW YORK

For Mathis and Hazel
—J.H.

For Marijka Kostiw,
for an outstanding collaborative effort,
and for my family
—E.F.

Text copyright © 2015 by Jennifer Hamburg • Illustrations copyright © 2015 by Edwin Fotheringham • All rights reserved. Published by Scholastic Press, an imprint of Scholastic Inc., *Publishers since 1920*. SCHOLASTIC, SCHOLASTIC PRESS, and associated logos are trademarks and/or registered trademarks of Scholastic Inc. • No part of this publication may be reproduced, stored in a retrieval system, or transmitted in any form or by any means, electronic, mechanical, photocopying, recording, or otherwise, without written permission of the publisher.
For information regarding permission, write to Scholastic Inc., Attention: Permissions Department, 557 Broadway, New York, NY 10012. • Library of Congress Cataloging-in-Publication Data • Hamburg, Jennifer, author. • Monkey and Duck Quack Up! / by Jennifer Hamburg ; illustrated by Edwin Fotheringham. — First edition. pages   cm • Summary: Monkey and Duck enter a rhyming contest but there is one problem—Duck cannot rhyme and all he says is "quack." • ISBN 978-0-545-64514-0 • 1. Monkeys—Juvenile fiction. 2. Ducks—Juvenile fiction. 3. Stories in rhyme. 4. Contests—Juvenile fiction. [1. Stories in rhyme. 2. Monkeys—Fiction. 3. Ducks—Fiction. 4. Contests—Fiction. 5. Rhyme—Fiction. 6. Humorous stories.] I. Fotheringham, Ed, illustrator. • II. Title. PZ8.3.H172Qu 2015 • [E]—dc23 • 2013035362 • 10 9 8 7 6 5 4 3 2 1   15 16 17 18 19 • Printed in Malaysia 108 • First printing, March 2015 • The text type was set in Gotham Rounded Medium and Gotham Rounded Bold. • The display type was set in Circus Mouse Black. • The illustrations were done in digital media. • Art direction and book design by Marijka Kostiw

Monkey spied the bright blue sign,

hanging from a nearby vine.

RHYMING CONTEST, ENTER NOW!

REGISTER WITH LOU THE COW.

FIND A FRIEND AND RHYME IN TWOS.

(Winners win a three-day cruise!)

Monkey screeched and turned to Duck.

"Buddy, ol' pal, are we in luck!

We can do this, we can rhyme!

We're young, we're hip, we're in our prime.

We'll find the perfect words to use,

and then we'll win a three-day cruise!"

"I'll say a rhyme,

you say one back.

Sound good to you?"

And Duck said,

"Quack."

"Beat! Sheet! Meet! Greet!

Eat some wheat,

then wash your feet!

Have a seat!

Trick or treat!

Hear a finch go tweet, tweet —"

"**Quack.**"

"No, no, no, you silly bird.

Saying 'quack' is just absurd.

Really, Duck, we cannot lose.

I want to win that

three-day cruise!"

Monkey puffed.

"Okay. Look, Duck.

Clearly you're a wee bit stuck.

Stand up straight and lace your shoes.

We MUST be on that three-day cruise!"

"Hope! Nope! Scope! Slope!

Please don't mope,

let's play jump rope!

Learn to lope!

Try to cope!

Take a bath with lots of —"

Monkey stared and Duck stared back.

"Any chance you won't say 'quack'?"

"Think of seagulls. Think blue skies.

Think about a pink sunrise

I can swim, and you can snooze —

BUT FIRST WE NEED THAT THREE-DAY CRUISE!"

"Pig! Jig! Twig!"

"Quack."

"Hug! Bug! Slug!"

"Quack."

"Feather! Weather! Leather!"

"Quack."

"Silly! Chilly! Hilly!"

". . . Quack."

Monkey cried, "There goes my dream!

I thought we'd be a rhyming team.

But 'quack, quack, quack' is all you say.

So we should just call it a day."

But then he figured out a way . . .

Up onstage, when it was time,

they wowed the crowd with one great rhyme:

"Rack! Sack! Plaque! Track!

Grab a snack and play blackjack!

Wash your back! Hug a yak!"

And Duck said . . .

One week later — FINALLY!

The winners reveled out at sea.

"Hey, Duck!" said Monkey with a grin.

"You know, I always knew we'd win."

"The two of us, we have a knack.

Don't you agree?"

And Duck said . . .